# Horse Happy

## A BRISA STORY

By Sibley Miller

Illustrated by Tara Larsen Chang and Jo Gershman

Feiwel and Friends

For Bunny—Sibley Miller

For Lizzie, princess extraordinaire!
—Tara Larsen Chang

For Savannah, my patient Percheron, who has taught
me what it means to have a horse as a friend
—Jo Gershman

A FEIWEL AND FRIENDS BOOK
An Imprint of Macmillan

Printed in China by South China Printing Co. Ltd.,
Dongguan City, Guangdong Province.
For information, address Feiwel and Friends,
175 Fifth Avenue, New York, N.Y. 10010.

Library of Congress Cataloging-in-Publication Data

Miller, Sibley.
Horse happy : a Brisa story / by Sibley Miller.
p. cm. — (Wind Dancers ; #2)
Summary: After seeing the human child, Leanna, argue with her
younger sister, the four tiny, winged horses leave their new home in an
apple tree for another adventure, but their day of berry picking is
spoiled by a fight of their own.
ISBN 978-0-312-38281-0
[1. Magic—Fiction.  2. Horses—Fiction.  3. Fighting (Psychology)—
Fiction.]  I. Title.
PZ7.M63373Hor 2008    [E]—dc22    2008012785

DESIGNED BY BARBARA GRZESLO
Feiwel and Friends logo designed by Filomena Tuosto

First Edition: 2008

5  7  9  10  8  6

mackids.com

# CONTENTS

## Meet the Wind Dancers

One day, a lonely little girl named Leanna blows on a doozy of a dandelion. To her delight and surprise, four tiny horses spring from the puff of the dandelion seeds!

Four tiny horses with shiny manes and shimmery wings. Four magical horses who can fly!

Dancing on the wind, surrounded by magic halos, they are the Wind Dancers.

The leader of the quartet is **Kona**. She has a violet-black coat and a vivid purple mane, and she flies inside a halo of magical flowers.

**Brisa** is as pretty as a tropical sunset with her coral-pink color and blond mane and tail.

Magical jewels make up Brisa's halo, and she likes to admire her gems (and herself) every time she looks in a mirror.

**Sumatra** is silvery blue with sea-green wings. Much like the ocean, she can shift from calm to stormy in a hurry! Her magical halo is made up of ribbons, which flutter and dance as she flies.

The fourth Wind Dancer is—surprise!—a colt. His name is Sirocco. He's a fiery gold, and he likes to go-go-go. Everywhere he goes, his magical halo of butterflies goes, too.

Every day, Leanna wishes she'll see the magical little horses again. (She's sure they're nearby, but she doesn't know they're invisible to people.) And, the Wind Dancers get ready for their next adventure.

## CHAPTER 1

# Home, Apple-Sweet Home

The Wind Dancers couldn't believe it—their first magical day on earth was coming to a close. And they had been *busy*.

They'd explored the meadows, forests, and farms of their new world.

They'd played with their magic—and they'd discovered what it's like to have too much magic.

And they'd made a beautiful little necklace for Leanna, the girl who brought them to life by blowing on a dandelion—

and that gift had made Leanna happy.

Now the four horses were flying into the darkening sky, enjoying their first sunset, and feeling their wings get heavy.

"I can't *wait* to get to bed," Brisa said, her pretty brown eyes looking sleepy.

"Me, too," Sumatra added. She stretched her front hooves and yawned a big yawn.

"Some shut-eye sounds awesome," Sirocco agreed. "There's just one problem: We *have* no beds!"

This stopped Brisa in mid-flight.

"Oh, *no*! I never thought about that!" she cried. "We don't have a home!"

Kona, of course, was quick to comfort everyone.

"There are plenty of cozy places we can stay," she assured her friends. "We can go back to Leanna's farmhouse and sleep on the porch. Or we can nest in the barn. Or we can make beds out of soft leaves in the garden. We'll be fine for tonight."

"Okay," Sirocco said. "But what about *eating* something first? I'm *starved*!"

Brisa suddenly clutched her empty belly with her pale hooves. Sumatra's stomach also rumbled, and Kona licked her dry lips.

"I guess we're all hungry," Kona said. "And parched. I didn't even realize it."

"Hey!" Sirocco chimed in. "I just remembered—I know where we can both eat *and* drink!" He darted toward a large, leafy apple tree in the middle of the meadow.

"C'mon," he called over his shoulder.

"These are the *juiciest* apples in the meadow. I had them for lunch!"

Kona, Brisa, and Sumatra dashed after Sirocco. By the time they arrived at the tree, Sirocco had already plucked a big red apple. He took a wet, noisy bite.

"*Whee!*" Brisa cried, diving down to a low branch and selecting a pinkish apple. "This one's as pretty as I am!"

"My turn!" Kona said. She alighted on a branch nearby and picked a rosy apple.

"Wait for me!" Sumatra yelled. She plunged into the tree's tangled branches in search of her own perfect piece of fruit.

Thunk!

*Chitter, chitter, squeak!*

Sumatra leaped back out of the apple tree, shaking her head woozily.

"I've crashed into something!" she neighed to her friends. "Something fat and furry!"

A moment later, a squirrel poked his offended furry face through the branches.

"Watch where you're flying, birdie, and who you're calling fat!" he said with a scowl. Then he took a closer look at Sumatra's sea-green mane and her fluttering wings. "Hey, wait a minute! *You're* not a bird. You're one of those magical flying horses!"

"You know about us?" Sumatra gasped.

"Definitely!" the squirrel said. "Word travels fast in the woods. The bees are always buzzin' with news, and the butterflies gossip at every flower."

The squirrel wrinkled his nose into a jowly smile. "I'm Gray. Anything you want to know about life on the meadow—I'm your squirrel."

"Nice to meet you, Gray," Kona said politely.

"So, how do you like them apples?" Gray asked the Wind Dancers. "Tasty, eh?"

"Delish!" Sirocco sighed. "I wish I could eat apples *every* day."

"Actually," Gray said, "that could be arranged."

He motioned to the Wind Dancers to follow him.

Giving each other curious looks, the tiny horses trotted along behind the squirrel. They crawled up one tree branch and down another. At last, they arrived at a hidden hole in the tree's upper trunk. Gray squirmed through the opening, and the horses followed.

Finally, they all stopped—and the Wind Dancers gasped!

They were standing with Gray inside a large empty room. The space had been neatly carved out of the tree's trunk. The tooth-marked walls were lined with windows, which were covered by tree-bark shutters.

Opposite the "front door" was another hole. This one was in the floor.

"That's the way to the floor below," Gray said, pointing at the hole. "There are four floors in all here."

"This is where you *live*?" Brisa asked, daintily kicking at an acorn shell on the floor.

"This is where I *used* to live," Gray said. "I've just finished hollowing out a new place in an oak tree nearby." He pointed at his sharp front teeth.

"Wow," Kona said. "That's impressive, being able to carve out a home for yourself with your teeth."

"Aw, it's no biggie," the squirrel said. "Anyway, if you want it, you can have it. Invite me over for apple pie every now and then, and we'll call it a deal."

"Really?" Brisa asked incredulously.

"Sure!" Gray said.

"All this tree house needs is a very good scrubbing," Kona added, nosing open one of the shutters and sweeping away some dust with her mane.

"We'll take it!" Sirocco yelled. He trotted over to the squirrel and gave him a friendly slap on the back with his hoof. "Thanks, Gray!"

"Enjoy," the squirrel said, heading for the door. "Stop by my new pad some time. I make a mean Acorn Crunch Cake."

After Gray left, Sirocco galloped through the tree house, exploring the other floors.

"It's huge!" he reported back to the fillies. "There's enough room on the bottom two floors for each of us to have our own stall. And we can eat in the floor above that. Gray made a rainwater spout that comes right through the wall. We can put a water trough underneath it. And this top floor can be our living room. We can pull in some apple bark and leaves and dandelion fluff to rest on."

"Bark?" Brisa asked quietly. "Leaves?"

"Yeah!" Sirocco said. "Neat, huh?"

"Um, I guess so," Brisa said even more quietly. "There's just one thing . . ."

"Well?" Sirocco demanded.

"It's just that this place is kind of . . . *ugly*!" Brisa cried.

She pointed at the bare, splintery floors and the tooth-scraped walls. "I just don't know if I can live in a *tree*. It's so dusty and *brown*. There's no beauty. No color. No . . . *mirrors*!"

Kona smiled.

"I think we can do something about that," she said. "Let's not forget—we *do* have our magic."

With that, Kona carefully tapped the floor next to the front door. Instantly, a bunch of pretty flowers appeared on the bare wood!

"This is called a 'throw rug,'" she explained to her friends. "I saw some in the yellow farmhouse where Leanna lives. It's pretty, isn't it?"

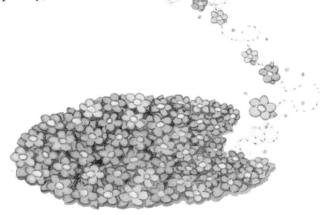

Next, Sumatra flew to the living room's windows, alighting at each one for an instant. When she was done, the windows were framed with her beautiful ribbons.

"Oh!" Brisa cried in delight. "Those are

lovely touches! Now me!"

She darted to the wall and began tapping jewels out of her magic halo. Soon, the wall was adorned with sparkling gems, including an extra-large clear jewel that was so shiny, Brisa could see her reflection in it.

"A mirror!" she sighed with a grin. After admiring herself for a moment, Brisa turned to her friends.

"Home, sweet home!" she said happily. "C'mon! Let's decorate the rest of the place."

In the kitchen, Sirocco made a table out of bark. Kona made some more flowery throw rugs, and Sumatra made some more ribbon-y window curtains.

Brisa, meanwhile, added another mirror to the wall.

Down in the horses' stalls, they wove sleeping blankets out of Sumatra's ribbons and fashioned dandelion fluff into pillows.

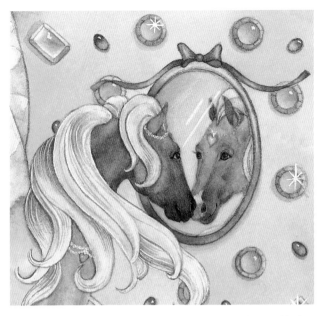

Kona made flower wreaths for each stall door and Brisa made . . . *more* mirrors! She whipped up one for each Wind Dancer, saving the biggest and shiniest for her own pink stall.

When the Wind Dancers went to sleep that night, their bellies full of apples and their backs warm beneath their ribbon-y blankets, nobody was happier with their cozy new home than Brisa.

. . .

Over the next few days, the Wind Dancers explored their world some more. They swam in the babbling creek that ran through the woods, and they ate picnics of apples.

They made friends with bees, chipmunks, and robins, sharing apples with them.

They rested in the highest branches of their apple tree at night, counting the stars and snacking on—what else?—more apples.

It was a very *apple-y* few days.

Which is why, as the Wind Dancers sat in the kitchen of their tree house a few mornings later, Brisa pushed her breakfast feed bucket away.

"What's wrong?" Kona asked. "You don't like my homemade applesauce? Maybe you should try an apple-spice muffin instead."

"The applesauce is delicious," Brisa said kindly. "It's just that . . . well, if I *eat* one more apple, or even *look* at another apple, I think I'm going to turn *into* an apple!"

"Brisa has a point," Sumatra said. "Some variety *would* be nice."

"I have an idea!" Kona replied. "Do you remember those blackberry bushes we saw the other day?"

"The ones on the other side of the woods?" Brisa asked. She had trotted over to the mirror she'd made on the wall and was now brushing her blond mane with a tiny currycomb. "The bushes with all the pretty red berries?"

"The berries were red because they weren't ripe yet," Kona explained. "But it's been a few warm, sunny days since then. Which means . . ."

"*Black* blackberries!" Sirocco yelled. "I bet those babies are really ripe and ready for picking now."

"Sounds like a perfect adventure for today," Sumatra added. "A scrumptious blackberry picnic!"

"We could bring blackberries home, too," Brisa suggested. "To make pies!"

"And jam!" Sirocco yelled.

"And muffins," Kona said with twinkling eyes. "Maybe we'll make extra for our animal friends, too."

"Oh, they'll be happy!" Brisa cried. "Let's get ready." She turned back to the mirror and held a couple of her jewels up to her blond mane.

"Do you think pink jewels will clash with the blackberries?" she asked her friends. "Should I go with blue?"

Sirocco snorted.

"This is your idea of getting ready, Brisa?" he sputtered. "We're going on a blackberry-picking trip, not to a beauty pageant!"

"You don't get it!" Brisa protested. "If today's the first day the berries are ripe, the blackberry patch will be teeming with birds and squirrels and raccoons and deer. It's going to be a *scene*. I have to look my best!"

Sirocco's mouth dropped open. Sumatra stifled a giggle, while Kona hid her smile by carrying the feed buckets to the water trough.

"If the berry patch is going to be *that* busy," Kona said, "I think we should head over there soon."

"Yeah!" Sirocco agreed, jumping up. "I'm already hungry for lunch!"

"Sirocco!" Sumatra whinnied. "You just took your last bite of breakfast!"

"You're right," Sirocco said with a nod.

"It's too early to think about lunch. I'll just
have a quick snack."

He nipped another apple muffin from the
table.

"Si-*ro*-cco!" Sumatra giggled.

But before Sirocco could reply, he was cut
off—by a high-pitched scream!

## CHAPTER 2

# A Sisterly Spat

"*Aaaah!* Take it back, Sara!"

The loud, angry voice came through the Wind Dancers' kitchen window. Curious, the horses tiptoed over and looked out to see what was going on.

Far below, they saw their friend Leanna. She was staring hard at another little girl—and looking mad!

The smaller girl had soft blond curls and brown eyes, just like Leanna.

And just like Leanna, the littler girl was squinting angrily. Her arms were crossed over her chest. And her mouth was squinched into a knot.

"They look just alike!" Sumatra said to the others. "I bet Sara is Leanna's little sister."

"I *won't* take it back," little-sister Sara was saying. "I said you were a big tattletale, and I meant it!"

"Am not!" said Leanna.

"Are too!" Sara said.

"Am *not*!" Leanna yelled.

"*Ahh!*" Sara screamed in frustration and stomped her tiny sneakered foot. "Stop saying 'am not,' when you *know* you are, too!"

"It's not tattling to tell Mom that you ate the entire bowl of cookie dough," Leanna said. "It was self-defense. She thought *I* ate it!"

"But you were eating blackberry jelly straight out of the jar last week," Sara said poutily. "And I didn't tattle on *you*, did I?"

"Only because Mom caught me," Leanna said, her cheeks pink with embarrassment. "So, you didn't get a chance. But you *would* have told on me if you could have."

"No, I wouldn't have!" Sara spat back.

"Oh, I can't listen to any more!" Brisa said to her friends, backing away from the window.

"I *know*," Sirocco agreed. "All that talk of cookie dough and jelly is making my mouth water!"

"I don't mean that!" Brisa said. "I mean the fighting. It's awful!"

"I wish we could help them," Kona said, shaking her head. "But being invisible to people, I don't know what we can do!"

So Kona went back to the trough to run rainwater over the sticky feed buckets.

Sirocco used his golden tail to sweep breakfast crumbs off the floor.

Sumatra began to weave a berry basket out of her magic ribbons.

And Brisa?

She went back to combing her mane.

As she watched her mane get smoother and shinier with every stroke, she nickered thoughtfully.

"*We* would never fight like Leanna and

Sara," she mused to her friends. "We're too happy for all that."

"Well," Kona said while she soaped up the feed buckets, "maybe Leanna and Sara aren't lucky enough to be as happy as we are."

"Still, fighting is mean," Sumatra said as she admired her brand-new ribbon-y berry basket.

"Fighting is ugly, too," Brisa declared. She turned back to the mirror and used her magic to pop a pink jewel onto her mane.

"Now *that's* pretty," she said, giving her mane a pat.

As Brisa admired her handiwork in the mirror, Leanna and Sara's fight drifted from her mind.

"Now that I think about it," Brisa said to herself, "I wonder if a *silver* jewel might make my eyes look more sparkly."

She combed the pink gem out of her mane and tried the silver.

"Ooh! Lovely!" Brisa breathed. "But what about blue?"

*Comb, comb, comb . . .*

Soon, the kitchen floor was littered with discarded jewels. But everyone was too busy to notice, until—

"*Ow!*"

Sirocco grunted in pain. He'd stepped on something hard and sharp. He peered beneath his throbbing hoof and saw on the floor—a pointy pink jewel!

"Hey!" he complained. Angrily, he kicked the jewel out of his way.

"*Ow!*"

This time, it was Sumatra who cried out— as the sparkling gem hit her right in the flank!

Sumatra dropped her berry basket on the floor and whirled around to glare at Sirocco. Her nostrils flared.

"Why are you mad at *me*?" she demanded of Sirocco.

"Huh?" Sirocco said absently. He was too busy frowning at his hurt hoof to even notice that the jewel had thwacked Sumatra.

"I *said*," Sumatra said irritably, "why did you kick that jewel at *me*? It was *Brisa* who dropped it."

"Hmm?" Brisa said. She thought she'd heard her name. But when she looked behind her, she only saw Sumatra glaring at Sirocco, and Sirocco glaring at his hoof. So she just shrugged and turned back to her mirror.

Meanwhile, Sumatra was getting more and more angry.

"Sirocco!" she said, galloping across the kitchen to get closer to the colt. "Are you even *listening* to me?"

She clopped her hoof on the wooden floor to get Sirocco's attention.

"Sumatra!"

*That* was Kona. She was standing at the trough, pointing at the floor beneath Sumatra's hooves.

"You're squashing my throw rug!" Kona

said exasperatedly.

Sumatra looked down. She was indeed trampling one of the pretty flower rugs that Kona had created for every room of the Wind Dancers' home. Sumatra frowned.

"Well, why'd you put your flowers on the floor," she asked Kona, "if you didn't want anybody to step on them?"

"*Stepping* on them is okay," Kona said. "Stomping the living daylights out of them is *not* okay!"

"Oh, whatever!" Sumatra scoffed. "They're *flowers*. They'll grow back!"

To prove her point, she stomped on the rug some more.

"Hey!" Kona yelled.

"*Grrrr,*" Sumatra growled.

"*Owwwww!*" Sirocco groaned.

And Brisa?

*Comb, comb, comb . . .*

"Okay, great!" she whispered to herself excitedly. "I think I've finally got *just* the right look for the blackberry patch."

Brisa had woven pink, silver, *and* blue gems into her mane. And, what's more, she'd alternated them with sleek little braids.

She turned away from her mirror and

looked at her friends. Sirocco was bent over, still hurting.

Kona and Sumatra were glaring at each other.

And the berry basket and the sudsy feed buckets had been completely forgotten.

"Aren't you horses ready yet?" Brisa asked with surprise. She trotted across the kitchen and scooped up the empty berry basket. "Gee, and you guys say that *I'm* the one who makes us late!"

The other Wind Dancers gaped at her. Then they glanced at each other and shook their heads.

"Oh, *Brisa*!" Sirocco muttered with a rueful laugh.

"What?" Brisa asked brightly.

"I think what Sirocco meant to say," Kona interjected with a weary smile, "was that you're right, Brisa. We'd best get going."

"Yay!" Brisa cried, fluttering her wings and heading for the kitchen window. "The blackberries await!"

CHAPTER 3
# Lost Cause

As the Wind Dancers flew toward the blackberry patch, they weren't as excited as they usually were.

Sirocco was still groaning over his hurt hoof.

Sumatra was still wincing over her bruised flank.

Kona was still scowling as she thought about how hard she'd worked on the kitchen's flowery rug.

And Brisa?

"*La, la, la!*" she sang. "Isn't it a beautiful

morning, you guys?"

"What'd you say?" Sirocco said. He glanced over at Brisa. As he did, he absent-mindedly veered off his flight path—and drifted *into* Sumatra's way!

To avoid crashing into Sirocco, Sumatra reared back, whinnying dramatically.

"Watch where you're going!" she yelled at Sirocco. "All I need is *another* injury from you."

"The way *you* fly?" Sirocco retorted grumpily. "*I'd* be the one in need of the ice pack."

"Now, now, you two," Kona interjected. Trying hard to stay cheery, she quickly changed the subject.

"Hey, look!" she said. "We've reached the forest. We're halfway there. Follow me to the blackberry patch!"

Kona turned to the right and began flying

along the edge of the woods. Brisa skimmed along behind her, still humming to herself, and Sirocco followed. But Sumatra stopped short, fluttering her wings in irritation.

When Kona realized that Sumatra wasn't following, she came to a halt herself.

"Is there a problem?" she asked Sumatra.

"I'm just wondering why *you're* always the leader," Sumatra said grumpily.

"Sumatra," Kona declared, "we know the blackberry patch is on the other side of the forest. The *only* way to go is around the trees."

"We could go *through* the forest," Sumatra countered. "It'd be much quicker."

"It'd also be a *great* way to get lost," Kona pointed out.

"Maybe we just need a new guide," Sumatra suggested sassily.

"Fine!" Kona said with a look of surprise. "If you know so much, *you* lead the way."

"Okay, I will!" Sumatra said with a satisfied grin.

She turned and plunged into the trees. The other Wind Dancers flew behind her until, only a couple minutes later, Kona spoke up.

"Don't you think we should veer north?"

she asked Sumatra. "At this rate, we're going to end up a mile from the blackberry bushes."

"See!" Sumatra burst out. She came to a halt. "I *knew* you couldn't just let me lead the way. You're bossy!"

"Am not!" Kona retorted.

Now Sirocco weighed in.

"Actually, Kona," he said, shooting Sumatra a mischievous wink, "you kind of, sort of *are*."

"Am *not*!" Kona insisted again.

And Brisa?

"*La, la, la!*" she sang as she admired the way the morning sun dappled the tree leaves. She barely took notice of Kona, Sumatra, and Sirocco.

Until, that is, they got too loud *not* to be noticed.

"Bossy!" Sirocco and Sumatra cried out together.

"Am not!" Kona yelled.

"Are too!" Sirocco and Sumatra replied.

"Hmm," Brisa said to herself. "This sounds kind of familiar."

But before she had a chance to ponder anymore, Sirocco broke in.

"Okay," he said to Kona. "If you want to prove that you can follow, follow *me*. Come on!"

Sirocco zipped off on a route that was

different from Sumatra's *and* Kona's. So they wouldn't lose sight of him, the fillies had no choice but to dart after him.

After ten minutes of veering around trees and leap-frogging over boulders, the Wind Dancers emerged on the other side of the forest.

"See?" Sirocco announced to the fillies with a big grin. "Here we are!"

"Um, actually," Sumatra said, looking around, "I *don't* see. There are *no* blackberry bushes here."

"She's right," Kona said, spinning in the air in search of the berry patch. "We're lost! We should have gone *my* way."

"Or *mine*," Sumatra sniped.

"You're both wrong," Sirocco argued. "If you'll just follow me, you'll see that the patch is in *this* direction."

He pointed to the left.

"No way!" Sumatra said. "It's *this* way."

Meanwhile, Brisa went her own way.

"*La, la, la!*" she sang cheerfully, as she flew along absent-mindedly. In fact, she flew *so* absent-mindedly that she careened into a big, leafy bush!

A big, leafy bush with big, fat, juicy berries all over it!

Brisa looked around. The bush was close to a babbling creek. It was clustered with a dozen more bushes just like it. And skittering and fluttering around all the bushes were squirrels, raccoons, birds, and bugs, all feasting on . . .

"Blackberries!" Brisa cried.

She flew back to the edge of the woods where she had last seen her friends.

"The blackberry patch!" she shouted, doing a backflip in the air. "It's right here!"

Kona, Sirocco, and Sumatra flew over to join Brisa and stared in surprise. Brisa had expected them to be as elated as she was. Instead, they seemed sulky and grumpy.

"You must be hungry after all that flying," Brisa said to them. "Being hungry can make a horse cranky."

She whizzed over to her bush and plucked four plump berries. She passed one to each of her friends, then kept the fourth for herself. She took a big gushy bite.

"See!" she said. "They're so sweet. Don't these berries make you feel great?"

"Well, mine was pretty yummy," Sirocco admitted grudgingly.

"Juicy, too," Sumatra added.

"Indeed," Kona said, with only a hint of frost in her voice.

"See, we all agree!" Brisa said joyfully. "It's lovely that we get along so well, don't you think?"

"Oh, *Brisa*!" Sumatra said, shaking her head and snorting.

"What?" Brisa asked brightly.

"I think what Sumatra meant," Kona sighed, "was that we had better get started on our blackberry picking."

"Yay!" Brisa cried. Singing to herself, she began to fly from bush to bush, looking for the prettiest berries.

Which is why she didn't notice that the flowers in Kona's halo were drooping. And why she didn't see that Sumatra's ribbon halo was sagging. And why she didn't know that Sirocco's butterflies were looking more frumpy than fluttery.

"*La, la, la,*" Brisa warbled. "This is such a *great* day!"

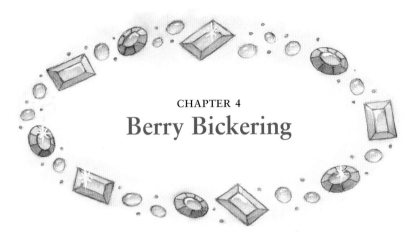

## CHAPTER 4

# Berry Bickering

Within minutes, the Wind Dancers were busy picking berries from Brisa's bush. Kona buzzed around the bottom.

"You find the *most* berries down here," she pointed out to her friends, "because nobody thinks to look near the bottom of the bush."

Sirocco laughed.

"Who cares about quantity?" he crowed. "I'm going for *quality*. And the *biggest* berries are the ones that get all the sun, the ones at the *top*!"

"Oh, anybody can pick berries from the top or bottom of a bush," Sumatra scoffed. She was rustling around deep inside the blackberry bush. "It's the blackberries on the *inside* that are the best. They're the juiciest, because they've been protected from *scavengers*."

She gave Kona and Sirocco pointed grins.

Kona and Sirocco snorted dismissively—just as Brisa flew around from the back of the bush, cradling a few berries in a leaf.

"Uh-oh, are you two catching colds?" she asked Kona and Sirocco.

"No!" Sirocco blurted. "Why would you think that?"

"I thought I heard you and Kona snorting," Brisa answered cheerfully.

Kona looked sheepish for a moment. But a triumphant whinny from Sumatra—who was still inside the blackberry bush—made her face go scowly.

"I suppose you think you've found the *perfect* blackberry in there," Kona called to Sumatra.

Sumatra nodded and held out a plump berry for the other Wind Dancers to see.

"It's so juicy, you could *drink* it instead of eat it," she boasted.

Since Kona didn't want to snort again, she merely rolled her eyes. Then she turned back to Brisa.

"What do *you* think is best: picking the biggest berries, the juiciest berries, or the *most* berries?"

"Oh, I don't care," Brisa said breezily, "as long as the berries are pretty! Look at *these*!"

She held out her leaf full of berries. They were as shiny as deep purple jewels.

"Aren't they beautiful?" Brisa asked dreamily. "I almost hate to eat them!"

"See?" Sirocco piped up from his perch at

the top of the bush. "Brisa agrees with me. A few great berries are better than a lot of *mediocre* ones."

He cackled as he eyed Kona's neat pile of berries on the ground next to the bush.

"What's mediocre about my berries?" Kona demanded. "They're just fine!"

"Hmm," Sumatra said. She grinned as she peeked out of the bush to regard Kona's berries. "They look a little *dry* to me."

Kona was trying to think up a clever reply when Brisa's sweet, tinkly voice cut her off.

"Hey!" Brisa called.

She was waving at her friends from the bank of the nearby creek, cooling her hooves in the water. She'd laid out a picnic "blanket" of smooth green leaves and divided her stash of pretty berries into four even piles. "It's time for our picnic!"

Kona couldn't help but smile at Brisa. She

grabbed some of her own berries, turned her back on Sirocco and Sumatra, and went over to join Brisa.

Sirocco's berries were so big, he could only carry two of them over to the picnic blanket.

"I'll eat one and give the other to Brisa," he whispered to himself. "If Kona and Sumatra think *their* berries are so great, they won't be interested in mine anyway."

Sumatra grabbed four of her juiciest berries and began to fly them over to the creek, too.

"These berries are super-duper juicy," she murmured to herself proudly. "Sirocco and Kona are *so* going to wish they'd picked them."

Unfortunately, the berries were *so* juicy that they squished between Sumatra's hooves before she'd even made it to the blanket. Juice spattered all over her forelegs and the ruined blackberries fell to the dirt with a *splat*!

"*Neeeiiiggh!*"

That was Sirocco, over by the creek. He was pointing at Sumatra's wrecked berries and laughing uproariously.

Sumatra's nostrils flared. Her lips clamped together. She could feel her face going red.

"This outing," she grunted, "has become *berry* annoying!"

. . .

The Wind Dancers *tried* to be happy as they sat down to their blackberry lunch. But for everyone except Brisa, that was pretty hard to do.

Sumatra ate Brisa's pretty berries, but she

deliberately avoided Kona's "dry" ones.

Sirocco chomped on his berries with his mouth open.

"Rude!" Sumatra whispered—but *not* so quietly that Sirocco couldn't hear.

And Kona made the others wash their hooves in the creek before eating, which Sirocco thought was silly.

"What's the fun of a picnic if you can't eat with dirty hooves?" he complained. "I *like* being dirty!"

But mostly, the Wind Dancers picnicked in stony silence. Even Brisa couldn't help but notice the tension.

And when Brisa *really* thought about it, she started to realize something . . .

She remembered how all three of her friends had looked as they hovered in the air at the edge of the woods, with their halos drooping.

*Were they all . . . fighting?* Brisa wondered, her eyes going wide.

But a moment later, she shook her head.

*That's impossible,* she assured herself. *We're a team. We're the Wind Dancers, and we love each other. And if you love each other, you* don't *fight!*

But just to make sure, Brisa decided to stay extra-close to her friends for the rest of the afternoon.

"I'm going to be the berry messenger," Brisa chirped to Kona, Sumatra, and Sirocco as they all flew back to the berry bushes.

Kona gave Brisa a small smile.

"That's very sweet of you," Kona said. "But are you sure? Picking berries is certainly more fun than hauling them to the basket."

"Which is why you should be happy!" Brisa cried, giving Kona a hug. "You get to do nothing but pick the berries all afternoon."

"I *am* happy," Kona said. But the flowers in her magic halo were still wilted. And her voice was tense as she looked at both Sirocco and Sumatra.

"Aren't we happy?" Kona prompted them with a motherly glare.

"Oh, sure," Sumatra said, returning Kona's glare. "I'm as happy as a bumblebee in a blackberry blossom."

Sirocco eyed Sumatra with a competitive gleam in his eye.

"Well, *I'm* as giddy as a tadpole who just sprouted legs," he said.

"Oh, yeah?" Sumatra challenged. "Then *I'm* as happy as a girl with a hundred ribbons in her hair."

"Okay, then," Kona piped up. "*I'm* as sunny as a field full of sunflowers."

Brisa giggled. Her friends were hilarious!

"I'm as bubbly as Brisa in a room full of mirrors," Sumatra added with a grin.

"Then *I'm* as happy," Sirocco said with a laugh, "as a pig rolling around in rotten watermelon rinds."

Suddenly, Sumatra's lip curled.

"Yuck, Sirocco," she scolded the colt. "That is disgusting!"

Kona frowned along with Sumatra, while Sirocco's laugh died abruptly.

*Oh no!* Brisa thought. *Just when things were lightening up—everyone's getting cranky again!*

She *had* to do something. Anything!

"Oooh! Look at that . . . um, *caterpillar*!" Brisa cried, pointing at a fat green bug that was chomping away at a nearby blackberry. "This patch is probably crawling with other hungry bugs, too. Maybe we should start picking blackberries again before they eat too many of them."

"Good point!" Sumatra said. She turned to the Wind Dancers' berry bush. "Look out, buggies, here I come!"

Sumatra plunged into the bush, knocking leaves in every direction.

Brisa winced. Making the horses compete with insects didn't seem like the *best* way to distract them from competing with each other. But at least it worked!

For a moment, anyway. But as soon as Brisa went to pick up a load of berries from Kona, it became clear that her friends were still snippy.

"Sumatra and Sirocco aren't picking more berries than I am, are they?" Kona asked Brisa.

"Um," Brisa said, "would it matter if they were?"

Kona didn't seem to hear her. She was too busy peering through the bush's leaves, trying to get a glimpse of the other horses.

"When you go to pick up their berries," Kona whispered to Brisa, "will you check to see how many they're getting?"

Brisa sighed as she dumped Kona's berries into the basket. Then she flew up to Sirocco at the top of the bush.

"You're going to need to make a *lot* of trips to carry these babies!" Sirocco crowed, pointing at the giant berries he'd stashed on a cupped leaf. Then he lowered his voice and asked Brisa, "There's no way Kona and Sumatra are finding blackberries that are this awesome, right?"

Brisa sighed some more.

Then she clawed her way into the middle of the bush to retrieve Sumatra's berries. When Brisa arrived, Sumatra had a question of her own for her.

"Don't you think we should separate *my* berries from Kona's and Sirocco's?" she asked. "They're so juicy, they're clearly the best ones for making blackberry jam."

Brisa heaved a third sigh.

"You know what?" she said. "I think it's time for us to go home."

"Oh, is our berry basket full yet?" Sumatra asked.

"Um, yes," Brisa answered. "Yes, you guessed it!"

She didn't want to tell Sumatra the truth— that all this competition was ruining the berry-picking outing for her.

Brisa and Sumatra flew down to the ground and called for Kona and Sirocco to join them. The basket was indeed groaning with berries—big ones and juicy ones and plentiful ones. Whoever carried the basket home was going to have quite a heavy load.

"Well, Kona," Sirocco suggested lightly, "you love being the leader, right? So I'm sure *you'll* want to carry the berry basket home."

"Oh, really?" Kona said, narrowing her

eyes at Sirocco. "Well, it just so happens that I'm tired. From picking so *many* berries, you know. I think *you* should carry the basket!"

"Have you forgotten?" Sirocco asked. He wiggled his sore front hoof at Kona and looked piteous. "*I* am jewel-struck."

That's when Sumatra jumped in.

"Oh, *I'll* give you struck!" she said with a cackle. She nipped a juicy berry out of the basket, then punted it at Sirocco.

*Splat!*

## CHAPTER 5
# Food Fight

"*Whoooa!*" Sirocco neighed in surprise.

Sumatra's berry had beamed him right in the face! Sirocco stood there for a moment, stunned, while dark berry juice dripped off his nose.

Then *he* dove for the berry basket.

Quickly snatching up one of his own big blackberries with his teeth, he tossed it into the air, then head-butted it at Sumatra. The berry *squelched* as it hit her—right on her bruised flank!

"*Eeek!*" Brisa cried. She flew high in the

air, afraid that flying berry juice might stain her pretty coat.

Meanwhile, Sumatra whinnied painfully.

"*Ow!*" she complained to Sirocco. "You hit my bad side on purpose."

"Oh, please," Sirocco scoffed. "I'm a *horse*, I'm not a baseball player. Horses can't aim."

"Oh, really? Horses can't aim, can they?"

*That* was Kona, her voice full of challenge.

Sumatra and Sirocco turned toward her. Kona was clutching two berries between her front hooves. She eyed the filly and the colt carefully, then used her forelegs to give each berry a kick!

*Splat! Splat!*

Sirocco and Sumatra were both hit.

"Right on target," Sumatra sputtered through the juice dripping off her forehead. "I'd expect nothing less from a *bossy horse*!"

"I am *not*!" Kona cried.

She used her tail to bat another berry at Sumatra. *Splat!*

Sumatra retaliated with a head-butted berry. But *her* berry ricocheted off of Kona's hoof and hit Sirocco in the belly. *Splat!*

From up above, Brisa tried to laugh.

"Food fights *are* fun, right?" she called down to her friends. "But, um, don't you want to save the berries for pie and jam?"

"Oh, *Brisa*!" Kona, Sirocco, and Sumatra said together. Then they returned to their berry brawl.

"Take *that*!" Sirocco yelled, beaning Sumatra with a berry. *Splat!*

"And *that*!" Kona cried, kicking another berry Sumatra's way. *Splat!*

"Don't forget the blackberry jam and muffins!" Brisa called anxiously.

The horses ignored her. *Splat! Splat! Splat!*

"You *guys*!" Brisa cried. She flew closer to her three friends, desperate for them to stop *splatting* each other.

And *that's* when it happened . . .

*Splat! Splat! Splat!*

Kona's berry hit Brisa right in the mane,

gunking up her
braids and
jewels.
Sirocco's berry
landed on Brisa's
hind leg. And Sumatra's berry hit her
smack-dab on her nose.

Brisa gasped. Her chest began to heave.
Her lips began to tremble.

And then . . .

"*Wahhhhhh!*" she wailed.

Tears streamed from Brisa's eyes, making
not-so-pretty trails through the blackberry
juice on her face. But for once, she didn't care
how she looked. She was *miserable*.

Brisa boo-hooed for a good minute before
she realized something.

The *splats* had ceased.

Kona, Sumatra, and Sirocco had stopped
yelling at each other.

And all three Wind Dancers were staring at her.

"You're *crying*!" Kona said.

"Brisa," Sirocco added, "I thought you said we were too *happy* to cry!" He looked squirmy and uncomfortable.

"No," Brisa corrected him. "I said we were too happy to *fight*. But guess what? We *are* fighting! Just like Leanna and her sister."

"It took you *this* long to realize that?" Sumatra said in wonder. "Oh, *Brisa*!"

"Yeah," Sirocco said. "What have *you* been doing all day while we were fighting?"

"Singing and being her usual happy self," Kona answered for her crying friend. "While the rest of us have been acting *horribly*."

"Well . . . well . . ." Embarrassed, Sumatra searched for an explanation. "Sirocco started it! This morning in the kitchen! He kicked a jewel at my flank!"

"That's because Brisa's jewel hurt my hoof!" Sirocco said. Hot, angry tears were gathering in his eyes.

"Well, you didn't have to take it out on me," Sumatra cried. She began to sob.

"But then *you* took it out on *me*," Kona said to Sumatra. Kona was teary now, too. "You stomped on my flowers. I think you should apologize."

"Well, *I* think Sirocco should apologize first," Sumatra said with a whimper.

"Fine!" Sirocco snapped. "I'm sorry . . . that I stepped on Brisa's jewel!"

"That doesn't sound like sorry to me," Sumatra sniffled.

"And, I'm still waiting for *my* apology," Kona said to Sumatra.

Brisa was shocked. She'd had no idea that this awful day had all begun with *her* stray jewel! So she jumped into the fray.

"If I started this," she said to her friends, "I should be the first one to say I'm sorry. Sirocco," she said, turning to the colt, "I wish I'd been more careful. If I hadn't dropped that jewel, you never would have stepped on it."

"And then, I guess I wouldn't have kicked it at Sumatra," Sirocco replied, giving Sumatra an apologetic look.

"And then I would have watched out for Kona's flowers," Sumatra said, shooting Kona a shy smile.

"And then," Kona added, "I wouldn't have been so bossy during our flight here."

"And *none* of you," Brisa said finally, "would have been so competitive about your blackberries! I'm sorry again, you guys!"

"*I'm* sorry, too," Sumatra echoed.

"So am I," Kona added.

"Me, too!" Sirocco responded.

"We're *all* sorry!" Brisa said jubilantly. "This is great! Group nose nuzzle, everyone!"

The four tiny Wind Dancers scrunched together for one big, forgiving hug. When they pulled away, they were all grinning big, blackberry juice-drenched grins.

Then Sumatra buzzed back over to the blackberry bush, plucked a few berries, and carried them over to the basket. Her happy ribbon halo buzzed, too.

"That's a good idea, Sumatra," Kona said generously, her flower halo perking up. "We lost a bunch of berries to the food fight. I'll help you refill the basket."

"And when we're done with the picking," Sirocco announced, "*I'll* carry the basket home." His butterfly halo danced happily around him.

"No, *I* will," Brisa offered.

"No, I should," Kona said.

"No, me!" Sumatra insisted.

"Wait!" Brisa cried out. "Let's not be so

nice to each other that we get into another fight!"

Which made all four Wind Dancers burst out laughing.

Now Brisa looked forward to the long flight home.

She felt *very* certain that Kona, Sumatra, and Sirocco would navigate the trip *together*.

Nobody would try to take control.

Nobody would get them lost.

And *all* of them, taking turns with the berry-filled basket, would make it home in time for blackberry pie and jam.

And they did.

## A Sweet Good-Night

The Wind Dancers hovered together outside Leanna's bedroom window. They'd had a giant dinner of blackberry pancakes, topped with blackberry jam, followed by blackberry pie. They were very full and very sleepy.

But they were also very excited.

"Look!" Brisa whispered. "There she is!"

Indeed, Leanna was walking into her bedroom just then. She yawned a big yawn as she snuggled under her covers. She, too, was pleasantly worn out.

She thought about everything she'd done that day. She'd visited with the horses at the farm nearby (the little gray filly was her favorite). And she'd climbed to the top of her favorite tree. And . . .

*Oh, yeah,* Leanna remembered. *And Sara and I had that fight out by the apple tree this morning. It's funny* now *how that seems like so long ago.*

"Leanna?"

Leanna glanced at her bedroom door. Sara was standing there, holding her favorite book.

"Want to read the story together?" Leanna offered her little sister.

Sara nodded eagerly and ran across the room. She dove under Leanna's covers and cuddled up against her.

Leanna read the first page and Sara the second, and so on.

As they neared the end of the story, their eyes grew heavy, and the book fell to the floor.

Just before falling asleep, Leanna thought of her little friends, the tiny, sparkly flying

horses: the Wind Dancers.

*I wonder what* they *did today?* Then she thought, *Maybe tomorrow I'll finally see them again!*

Outside the bedroom window, Brisa reached into the berry basket, which she was carrying around her neck, and gently used her teeth to pull out a warm bundle. Inside were two tiny blackberry pies.

"Mmm!" Sirocco said, giving the pies a

blissful sniff. "Are you sure I can't have just a tiny little bite?"

"Sirocco!" Kona scolded. "Those pies are a present. And besides, didn't you eat *enough* berries today?"

"*I* sure did," Sumatra said, clutching her full belly.

"Yeah," Brisa agreed, nudging the pies onto Leanna's windowsill. "In fact, I think if I eat one more blackberry, I'm going to turn *into* a blackberry!"

"Maybe," Kona said with a laugh, "we should have *apples* for breakfast tomorrow."

"Not to mention another adventure!" Brisa replied.